CONT:

The Characters   4

Mahabharata
The final battle SOLD   7

Taking things further   55

THE CHARACTERS

Draupadi

This most beautiful of women married the five great warriors, the Pandavas, but was humiliated by Duryodhana, their Kaurava cousin. Can war between the Pandavas and Kauravas redress this wrong?

Krishna

Lord Krishna, the ninth avatar of Lord Vishnu, has sworn not to take up weapons in the great war of Kurukshetra. But does he support both sides equally? Will he be forced to join in the fighting?

Bhishma

This selfless patriarch and mighty warrior of the Kuru dynasty loves both the Kauravas and the Pandavas. Which side will he fight for when war comes?

Yudhishtira

The eldest of the Pandavas was king of his own land, Indraprastha, until his cousin Duryodhana cheated him of it. Will he ever get back his title and his lands?

Abhimanyu

Abhimanyu is the young son of Arjuna. As famous an archer and warrior as his illustrious father, will he come safely through the war?

Karna

Born to a princess and the Sun God, yet fated to grow up in a charioteer's home. Unrivalled in archery, yet fated to forget his skills in a crisis, will he survive the war?

Aswathama

A brave warrior, trained by his father Drona, he treacherously slaughters the Pandavas' sleeping children. Will he ever redeem himself?

5

THE FAMILY TREE OF THE KURU RACE

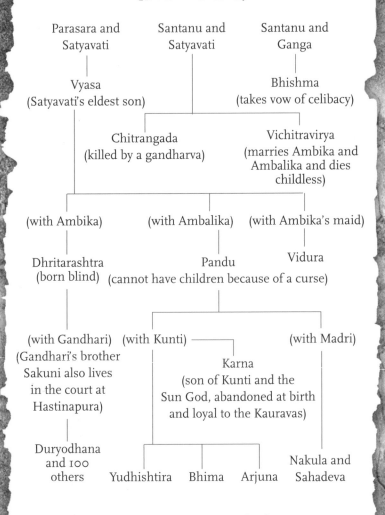

Parasara and Satyavati

Santanu and Satyavati

Santanu and Ganga

Vyasa
(Satyavati's eldest son)

Bhishma
(takes vow of celibacy)

Chitrangada
(killed by a gandharva)

Vichitravirya
(marries Ambika and Ambalika and dies childless)

(with Ambika)

(with Ambalika)

(with Ambika's maid)

Dhritarashtra
(born blind)

Pandu
(cannot have children because of a curse)

Vidura

(with Gandhari)
(Gandhari's brother Sakuni also lives in the court at Hastinapura)

(with Kunti)

(with Madri)

Karna
(son of Kunti and the Sun God, abandoned at birth and loyal to the Kauravas)

Duryodhana and 100 others

Yudhishtira

Bhima

Arjuna

Nakula and Sahadeva

Gandhari's 101 children are called The Kauravas
Kunti's and Madri's 5 children are called The Pandavas

MAHABHARATA
THE FINAL BATTLE

The rivalry between the royal cousins the
Pandavas and the Kauravas, that had started
when they were children, was coming to a
head. Everyone in the kingdom of Bharata
knew that war was in the air.

Krishna, friend to the Pandavas and the
Kauravas alike, set out for Hastinapura, the
Kauravas' capital, to mediate. He was accorded
a grand welcome by Duryodhana, the eldest
Kaurava brother. That evening at the Kuru
court, before all the elders including Bhishma
and the Kauravas' aging father Dhritarashtra,
Krishna explained why he was there.

'I have come as a well-wisher of both
branches of your family, to remind you of what
happened in this court thirteen years ago. A
wager was proposed and accepted for a game
of dice. The loser was to be exiled to the forest

for twelve years and to live for a further year without being discovered. The winner was to enjoy the land of the loser for that period. Yudhishtira, eldest of the Pandavas, lost the game, and went to live in the forest with his brothers and his wife. Then they lived for a further year without being discovered by the Kauravas. Under the terms of the wager, the Pandavas are now entitled to have their land back.'

Duryodhana argued that the Pandavas had been found before the end of the year of hiding and so must return to the forest for another twelve years. 'Under no circumstance shall I give back the land,' he said. 'The Pandavas were never entitled to any portion of the country anyway. It belongs to Dhritarashtra, my father, and after him it comes to me.'

Krishna entreated the recalcitrant prince to think again. 'I come on a mission of peace,' he said, 'but the Pandavas will go to war if they

do not get their due. Yudhishtira is willing to forego half of the land he is entitled to. He will settle for five villages if that will keep the peace.'

'They shall not have even five houses,' Duryodhana said contemptuously. 'I shall not give up the space occupied by the point of a needle. Go and tell this to Yudhishtira.'

Krishna was not prepared to give up so easily. 'Duryodhana, you know that your claim is not a true one. Give it up now.'

This angered Duryodhana. He called out, 'Soldiers, come and tie up this impudent messenger.' The elders, Drona, Bhishma, Vidura and Gandhari all pleaded with Duryodhana to stop.

Krishna was no ordinary messenger. He was the avatar of Lord Vishnu, the preserver of the universe, born on earth to destroy evil and restore dharma. As the soldiers advanced towards Krishna, a dazzling light filled the court and the soldiers turned away, blinded.

Bhishma, Drona and Vidura saw Krishna in his vishwaroopa, the divine form that held the whole universe within it. Even the blind Dhritarashtra briefly saw the grand vision. He quickly called the soldiers back, and apologised on behalf of his son.

Krishna returned to the kingdom of Virata where the Pandavas awaited his arrival, hoping for good news.

But there was no good news. War was now inevitable, and both sides made preparations. The Pandavas and the Kauravas sent messengers to neighbouring kingdoms, asking their rulers to join them in the war. Both Duryodhana and Arjuna approached Krishna for support.

'I don't approve of this war,' said Krishna,

'so I shall not fight in it. But both of you came to me for support, so I will help both of you. One of you can have my highly trained army, and the other can have myself but without any weapon. As Arjuna is the younger, he shall choose first.'

Arjuna gladly chose Krishna without any weapon, and Duryodhana equally gladly accepted the mighty army of Krishna, which was famed for its great skill with weaponry.

Though the elders, Bhishma, Drona and Vidura, were fond of the Pandavas, they owed their allegiance to the throne of Hastinapura. Their affection for the Pandavas might keep them from killing them, but they would have no qualms about trying to defeat them. As for Karna, the peerless warrior, he knew that

the Pandavas were the enemies of his friend
Duryodhana and must be destroyed.

The Pandavas' mother, Kunti, and the
Kauravas' mother, Gandhari, were both
saddened by the thought of their sons fighting
what they knew would be a fight to the end. Both
dreaded the sorrow of losing their children.

Kunti was tormented by the thought that her
sons were fighting on opposing sides. Karna
had been born to Kunti before her marriage
and abandoned at birth. His father was the Sun
god. Kunti decided that she would risk Karna's
anger and bitterness and reveal the secret of
his birth to him. She would tell him that she
was his mother and so the Pandavas were his
brothers. He would surely not want to kill his
own brothers if he knew the truth.

She went early next morning to where Karna offered his daily puja to his father, the Sun god. Kunti had heard that during this time Karna would refuse no request made to him. Unable to bear the dazzling light and the heat of the sun's rays, she stood in Karna's shadow, finding pleasure, even in her predicament, in the nearness of the son she had given up so long ago.

Karna finished his puja and turned to see an old woman standing behind him. He looked closely and saw that it was Kunti, standing like a supplicant before him.

'Why is the Queen Mother, the mother of the mighty Pandavas, standing humbly before me?' he asked.

Kunti replied, 'I am not just the mother of the Pandavas, I am also the mother of Karna. I am the unfortunate woman who gave birth to you, and had to give you up. I have come seeking alms.'

Anger and bitterness welled up in Karna. 'All these years I have called the wife of the charioteer who brought me up "mother". It is rather late to find the mother who gave birth to me. But I cannot refuse anyone's request at this time of the day, so what can I do for you, Queen Mother?'

'I cannot bear the thought of my sons killing each other,' said Kunti tearfully. 'Leave Duryodhana and join your brothers. Once they know who you are, they will welcome you and make you their king, for you are their eldest brother. You belong with them.'

Karna said gently, 'When the Pandavas insulted me at the young princes' graduation ceremony, it was Duryodhana who came to my rescue. He gave me a kingdom and saved my pride. Now, when he is about to fight a war, I cannot desert him. You must forgive me for refusing to do what you have asked.'

Seeing the sadness in Kunti's face, Karna

added, 'However, your coming here shall not
be in vain. I promise you that I shall not kill
my brothers, Yudhishtira, Bhima, Nakula and
Sahadeva. Arjuna and I are fated to meet in combat,
and only one of us will survive. You, mother, will be
left with five sons at the end of the war.'

Kunti went away, worried about the duel to
come between Arjuna and Karna, but relieved at
the thought that her other sons would not die at
the hands of their elder brother.

Both sides held councils of war to elect their
commanders. In the Pandava camp, it was
decided that Dhrishtadyumna, Draupadi's
brother, should command their forces.

In the Kaurava camp, Bhishma was elected
commander, but not without dissent. Karna
questioned the commitment of the elders. He

accused them of being half-hearted in their
support of Duryodhana and partial to the
Pandavas.

Bhishma was very angry. 'It is your
arrogance and ill-considered advice that have
brought us to this pass. A good advisor does
not encourage his king to go against dharma,
yet this is what you have done time and again.'

Karna walked out in a rage. 'I shall not
fight alongside Bhishma. As long as he is
commander, I shall stay out of this war.'

Karna's decision was a terrible blow to
Duryodhana, but he knew that Karna was a
devoted ally, and trusted that he would be there
when the need came. Duryodhana also knew
that Bhishma's position as commander could
not be questioned.

So the lines of battle were drawn. The Kaurava army was larger than that of the Pandavas. They fielded eleven battalions against the Pandavas' seven. Yet the warriors on the Pandava side were fully convinced of the righteousness of their cause, while many Kaurava supporters were there only from a sense of duty.

The rules of warfare were strict. A warrior who was disarmed could not be attacked. Battle commenced at sunrise and finished at sunset. After that, both armies could see to the care of their wounded and the cremation of their dead.

The first day of the war dawned in Kurukshetra, where the fighting was to take place. Duryodhana sought the blessings of his parents. The blind Dhritarashtra blessed his son. 'Go forth and win. I have been granted a boon that my messenger can go untroubled anywhere in the battlefield and report what he has seen. I shall know what is happening at all times. May victory be yours.'

But when Duryodhana went to seek his mother's blessing, Gandhari said, 'May victory bless the righteous.'

The two armies were arrayed in the battlefield, the sun glinting on their weapons. Krishna, who had sworn that he would not fight, had decided that he would be Arjuna's charioteer; he was seated with a whip in one hand and the reins of the horses in the other. Conches were blown by the heroes on both sides, their sound both an auspicious sign and a challenge to the enemy.

Moments later, the Pandavas were horrified to see Yudhishtira laying down his weapons, getting down from his chariot, and walking towards the Kaurava army. 'Is our elder brother going to surrender before the battle starts?' Bhima muttered.

But Yudhishtira paid no attention and went straight to Bhishma's chariot, bowed before him, and sought his blessings. Bhishma blessed him with affection and sent him away.

Yudhishtira next went to Drona, and then to the other Kuru elders. After obtaining their blessings, he returned to his chariot and took up his weapons.

The battle was soon raging fiercely. Each man's mission was to bring as much death and destruction to the enemy side as he could.

That is, all but one warrior. 'How can I kill Bhishma, who has been like both father and grandfather to me? And Drona, who has taught me everything that I know and loves me more than his own son? Am I to kill my uncles and cousins?' Arjuna, the invincible warrior, found that he could not fight. He turned to Krishna. 'Krishna, my arms feel weak and my bow falls from my hand. I cannot fight my own relatives. It cannot be right to kill so many loved ones for the sake of land. It is a sin. Let me go back.'

'Do not despair, Arjuna', said Krishna. 'It is your duty to fight and to rid this earth of evil. Sin lies in not doing your duty. Do what you must without greed or desire. That is the sign of a truly noble human being.' Krishna spoke to Arjuna at length on the nature of the immortal soul, the nature of duty, of karma and the universe. This divine knowledge

imparted by Krishna on the battlefield is known
as the Bhagavad Gita, the divine song, the most
sacred of knowledge.

His resolve strengthened by Krishna's divine
counsel, Arjuna picked up his weapons again
and went forth into battle. Instead of going to pay
respects to each of the elders as Yudhishtira had
done, he sent arrows humming past the ears of
Bhishma and Drona in greeting, and sent arrows
to fall at their feet in obeisance.

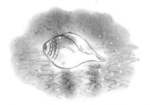

The battle raged. At the end of the first day
the honours lay with the Kauravas. Wherever
Bhishma's chariot went, destruction followed.
Innumerable noble warriors on the Pandava side
had fallen to the old hero's arrows. The soil was
seeped in blood.

By the end of the second day, however, the
Pandavas had the upper hand. Arjuna's young

son, Abhimanyu, was proving himself a warrior equal to his father.

Duryodhana was far from pleased at the Pandavas' success, and suspected that Bhishma, Drona and the other Kuru elders were not putting their hearts into the battle. He went to Bhishma and complained. 'Sir, we have the larger army, but we seem to be losing the war. Are you on their side?'

Bhishma replied in sorrow. 'Son, I tried to prevent this war with all the wise words at my disposal. However, once war was declared I said I would fight on your side. Yet our cause is not just, and perhaps that weakens me. The Pandavas know that their cause is righteous and are strengthened by that certainty. I am fighting wholeheartedly. It is only against the warrior Sikhandi that I cannot fight. He was born a woman and raised as a man. I do not fight against women.'

Long ago, Bhishma had prevented the beautiful Amba from marrying the man she loved. Dejected, she had given up her life, praying that in her next life she would be able to kill Bhishma. Thus she was reborn as Sikhandi, whose sole purpose was to help bring about Bhishma's destruction.

On the Pandava side, a worried Krishna said, 'Arjuna, you are not fighting with all your heart. If you want to win this war, you must kill Bhishma. This is not the time to remember how fond he is of you. Now he is your enemy.'

On the tenth day of the war, Krishna placed Arjuna's chariot behind Sikhandi's. He knew that Bhishma would not attack Sikhandi, leaving Arjuna safe and free to attack Bhishma.

The battle between the two great warriors of the Kuru clan, Bhishma and Arjuna, waged long and fierce. Other warriors stopped fighting to watch the skill of the two. Bhishma was

handicapped by the presence of Sikhandi
between them. Overpowered by Arjuna, his
body pierced with arrows, Bhishma fell. He
lay, the gallant Bhishma, a few feet above the
ground, on a bed of arrows.

The fighting stopped when Bhishma fell.
Friend and foe alike rushed to the place where
he lay. Though his body was supported by the
arrows, Bhishma's head hung down. He said,

'I am uncomfortable with my head hanging down like this. Raise my head for me.'

He looked at Arjuna. 'Son, make me comfortable.' Arjuna sent three arrows into the ground, positioning them so that they supported Bhishma's head.

The old man next asked for water. Another arrow went into the earth and a cold stream of water sprang up to moisten the fallen hero's lips. It was Ganga herself, come to quench the thirst of her son.

Bhishma addressed the crowd. 'I will choose the time of my death,' he told them, 'and it will not be yet. Return to your camps.'

Now that Bhishma had fallen, the Kauravas needed a new commander. Though Duryodhana felt the loss of the great fallen warrior, he found something to cheer him in that loss. Karna, who had stayed out of the fighting until now, would take up arms. Duryodhana knew that Karna was a warrior to rival Bhishma, and that his loyalty was beyond question.

Karna suggested that Drona, the guru who had taught the arts of war to all the cousins, be installed as commander.

That night Karna went quietly to the fallen Bhishma. He approached with trepidation and said, 'Sir, the son of Radha seeks your pardon and your blessings.'

Bhishma said, 'You are not the son of Radha, but the son of Kunti. Join your brothers. Without your support, Duryodhana will withdraw from this destructive war.'

Karna replied, 'You felt that the Pandavas had right on their side. And yet you fought for the Kauravas because of your loyalty to Hastinapura. I owe my loyalty to Prince Duryodhana and must fight for him. Please bless me.' And Bhishma blessed Karna.

The next day Duryodhana asked Drona to capture Yudhishtira alive. With the eldest Pandava alive but captive, the war could come to an honourable end.

So on the eleventh day of the battle Drona deployed his forces cleverly, and isolated Yudhishtira. But Arjuna arrived just in time to foil the attempt.

The Kauravas held a council of war and decided that Arjuna would be kept away the next day by a great force of warriors called 'samsaptakas' or the 'cursed ones' who had sworn to die in battle.

Thus on the twelfth day of the war the leader of the samsaptakas challenged Arjuna to fight. Arjuna could not in honour refuse, though he knew that he was needed to protect Yudhishtira. He arranged a force of warriors to guard Yudhishtira and took up the challenge. The battle raged fiercely, and it seemed to Arjuna that there was no end to the army he opposed. To kill a hundred of them was only to face another two hundred.

The Kaurava army made full use of Arjuna's absence and launched a fierce assault on the forces protecting Yudhishtira. A relentless Drona fought his way close to the eldest Pandava.

At that moment Arjuna shrugged off the remaining samsaptakas and rushed back to Yudhishtira. He and the other Pandavas managed to stave off Drona's attack until sunset brought the day's battle to an end.

That night Duryodhana reproached Drona. 'You said you would capture Yudhishtira today, and you almost succeeded. What prevented you? Was it that you remembered that you love the Pandavas more than you love me and my brothers?'

'I told you that Arjuna must be kept engaged elsewhere if I was to capture Yudhishtira,' Drona replied. 'Arjuna was back by the time I got within reach of Yudhishtira. If you keep him away tomorrow, I shall do as I have promised.'

The next day, the thirteenth of the war, the samsaptakas again challenged Arjuna, and again drew him away from the main action of the battle.

The Kaurava army arranged themselves in the shape of a many-petalled lotus; it was a skilled warrior who knew how to break that strong formation. Arjuna knew how to do it, but Arjuna was not there. Yudhishtira called Abhimanyu, Arjuna's son, and asked him,

'Do you know how to pierce the lotus formation?'

Abhimanyu told his uncle, 'I know how to enter the formation, but not how to come out of it. If I am followed by a force large enough to help me break out again, I can try.'

The soldiers assured Abhimanyu that they would stay close behind him, and he set off at full tilt towards the opposing army. He managed to break through the formation, but the Kauravas, led by Jayadratha, Duryodhana's brother-in-law, closed behind him. Now Abhimanyu was isolated behind enemy lines.

Though alone in the midst of his enemies, Abhimanyu fought bravely, sending Duryodhana scurrying for shelter and breaking Karna's armour. Finally the Kauravas had had enough. The veteran Kaurava warriors – Drona, Duryodhana and Karna – joined forces to attack the young boy.

Unable to bring Abhimanyu down even then, they killed his charioteer and his horses.

They destroyed his chariot, forcing him
to stand on the ground and fight. Drona's
arrow broke Abhimanyu's sword. Karna's
arrow destroyed his shield. Weaponless and
desperate, the youth lifted his chariot wheel
and used it as a weapon. Eventually the
combined onslaught of his opponents felled
him to the ground. Even as he struggled to his
feet again, he was struck dead. The rules of fair
play in warfare suffered a great blow that day.

After another day of fighting the samsaptakas,
Arjuna finally managed to destroy them all.
He returned to the camp, and was relieved to
find that Yudhishtira had not been captured.
Yet everybody was very quiet and sad. 'What
has happened that all of you are so silent?' he
asked.

When Yudhishtira reluctantly told him about Abhimanyu's death, Arjuna's sorrow knew no bounds. When he found out how cruelly his son had been killed, this sorrow turned to anger. The bereaved father swore, 'It was due to Jayadratha that my son was killed so wickedly. He shall not live to see the next sunset. If he does I shall end my own life.'

Both camps had spies listening in on the enemy, so news of Arjuna's oath reached the Kauravas that same evening. They decided to surround Jayadratha with their best warriors.

The next day, the fourteenth of the war, Arjuna set out to find Jayadratha. He was not surprised to find his way barred by Kaurava warriors.

First Drona stopped Arjuna and challenged him. 'You must defeat me before you can reach

Jayadratha.' The fight was short and decisive. Arjuna disarmed Drona, the teacher who had taught Arjuna the arts of war, and charged onwards.

Next Arjuna met Duryodhana, who also tried to stop him, but after another fierce fight Arjuna continued on his way. Thus the day continued, with Arjuna fighting and defeating warrior after warrior.

The Kauravas took heart from the fact that the sun was sinking low in the western sky. If they protected Jayadratha until evening, all would be well.

Krishna knew that it was time to intervene. If Jayadratha stayed hidden away among the other warriors until sunset, Arjuna would have to honour his oath by ending his own life.

Krishna summoned his divine weapon, the sudarsana chakra, to hide the setting sun. The sky darkened as if night had fallen. Surprised by the sudden darkness, Jayadratha lifted his head to check whether the sun had actually set. As Jayadratha raised his head above his guards, Krishna pointed him out to Arjuna. Arjuna did not hesitate for a second. A single arrow was swiftly despatched, severing Jayadratha's head.

That night Krishna told the Pandavas that they must find a way to deal with Drona. It was difficult to defeat this master of weapons by fair means; some trick must be used. Drona's greatest weakness was his son Aswathama. The Pandavas knew that Drona could not survive his son's death.

The next day, the fifteenth of the war, Bhima killed an elephant called Aswathama. Bhima then went close to Drona's quarters and declared loudly, 'I have killed Aswathama.'

Drona was horrified, but needed proof of what he had just heard. He asked Yudhishtira, who was known to be incorrigibly truthful, whether the news was true.

Yudhishtira replied, 'Yes, Aswathama has been killed.' But he could not bear to utter a lie and added quietly, 'Aswathama, the elephant.' Krishna blew his conch loudly to drown Yudhishtira's voice and prevent Drona from hearing the truth.

Grief-stricken and drained of any desire to fight, or even to live, Drona put down his weapons. Seizing the moment, Dhrishtadyumna, commander of the Pandava army, killed him.

Thus the life of this great warrior, the guru who had taught both the Pandavas and the Kauravas the skills of war, came to an end.

With Bhishma and Drona dead, Karna was now the Kauravas' only hope. But it was a Karna shorn of his golden armour and earrings who led the Kaurava warriors in battle.

Indra, the king of gods and Arjuna's father, was fearful of Karna's invincibility and concerned for Arjuna's safety. Disguised as a brahmin, Indra approached Karna at his morning prayers, asking for his armour and earrings.

Karna knew that without his armour he would lose his invincibility. Yet he tore it off unflinchingly and handed it to the cunning Indra. Now he was as vulnerable as any ordinary mortal.

Arjuna and Karna confronted each other, while Bhima faced Dussasana, brother of Duryodhana. The mighty Bhima's anger was inflamed by his memory of events long ago, when Dussasana had dragged Draupadi by her hair and insulted her. Bhima killed Dussasana, then broke each of his limbs. Bhima collected Dussasana's blood to fulfil his oath of anointing Draupadi's hair with the blood of the man who humiliated her.

Karna was true to his promise to his mother Kunti, and spared the lives of his brothers even when he had the chance to kill them. But the battle between Karna and Arjuna was fought so fiercely, the skill of the two warriors so equal, that it is said that the gods came out of the heavens to watch it.

Arrows flew so fast and thick that they hid the sun, and the battlefield was bathed in shade. After a while Karna's chariot wheel sank into the bloody mire. Karna jumped down to lift the wheel, reminding Arjuna that chivalry demanded he refrain from attacking a defenceless warrior.

It was Krishna rather than Arjuna who replied. 'You speak of chivalry now when you need help. But where was this chivalry when Draupadi was dragged into the court? Where was it when Sakuni cheated at dice, when Duryodhana broke his word about returning the kingdom to the Pandavas? And, worst of all, where was this chivalry of yours when the young unarmed Abhimanyu was attacked and killed?'

Arjuna had hesitated to attack his
grounded foe, but at the mention of his
beloved Abhimanyu he took up an arrow
and let it fly. Karna fell. Thus died one of the
greatest heroes of Mahabharata, fated from
birth to lead an unhappy life but loyal to his
friend Duryodhana to the last.

When Duryodhana heard about Karna's death,
he grieved more than he had grieved for his
own slain brothers. The elders advised him to
give up this pointless war and sue for peace.

'There was a time for that,' he said, 'but
now, with so many of my brothers and friends
dead, how can I try for peace so that I can live?'

So the battle continued. Many more
warriors died on both sides, but the Kauravas
had the worst of it. Duryodhana sought relief

from the intense heat of battle in a nearby pond. He was followed by the Pandavas, who laughed at him, saying he had run away from the fighting.

The proud prince rose out of the water, ready to face his enemies. The Pandavas offered him the choice of single combat with any one of them, and Duryodhana chose Bhima, the only one he considered worthy of him. The cousins fought with maces, knowing that this was a fight to the death.

Krishna, who watched from the sidelines, reminded Bhima of the oath he had taken to break Duryodhana's thighs by a slap on his own thigh. Bhima remembered how Duryodhana had insulted Draupadi and hit him on his thighs, breaking them. This was against the rules of combat by mace, where all attacks had to be above the waist. Duryodhana fell to the ground.

Aswathama heard of Duryodhana's fate and the base way Bhima had felled him. Blinded by anger, Aswathama took an oath to destroy the Pandavas once and for all.

That night he stole into the Pandava camp. Weariness and grief had taken their toll, and what remained of the army slept deeply.

First Aswathama killed Dhrishtadyumna, who had slain Drona, his father. Then he killed all of Draupadi's sons. He could not find the

Pandava brothers, so set fire to their tents. The raging fire killed a large number of warriors, leaving only a handful of survivors.

Aswathama crept away, elated at his work. He came to where the wounded Duryodhana lay and said, 'I have killed most of the survivors of the Pandava army. Those I could not kill by weapon have died in the fire.'

Duryodhana thanked him, and said he could now die in peace. This fearless warrior and generous friend, defiant to the end, breathed his last on the battlefield at Kurukshetra.

Back at the Pandava camp, Draupadi surveyed the devastation. Her grief knew no bounds. She had lost her brother and her sons to Aswathama's dastardly attack. Only her husbands had survived.

The Pandavas set out to seek revenge on Aswathama. Arjuna drew his most fearsome weapon, the brahmastra. Aswathama too, drew his own brahmastra. If the brahmastras met the world would come to an end.

Fearing this, Krishna hurried to intervene before it was too late. He reached the warriors just as they drew their bows.

Withdrawing a brahmastra that had been set on its course required far more strength than to stop it before it left the bow. When Krishna ordered both combatants not to fire their brahmastras, Arjuna managed to draw back his and so avert disaster. Aswathama, however, failed.

It was too late. The brahmastra was sent with the instruction to destroy the race of the Pandavas. It went into the womb of Abhimanyu's wife and killed the unborn child that lay there. But Krishna breathed new life into the child and brought it back from death.

Aswathama admitted defeat. He had been given the blessing of eternal life and that became a curse now as he roamed the world friendless and grieving.

The great war of Kurukshetra had raged for eighteen days, and when it ended there were few survivors. The war that had been fought according to the rules of chivalry to begin with slowly degenerated into one where all rules were discarded for the sake of victory or revenge.

Those who survived realised too late that war brings loss and sadness not just to the vanquished, but to the victorious as well. Duryodhana was dead, but his parents were still alive. Long ago, Gandhari had bound her eyes with a piece of cloth so that she could

share her blind husband's fate. Now, for the first time since she had married, Gandhari removed the binding from her eyes so she could look at her sons as they lay dead on the battlefield.

She turned to Krishna and cursed him. 'You could have stopped this carnage if you had wanted to, but you did not. May you too suffer the loss of sons and relatives.'

Krishna smiled gently and said, 'Even your curse is as sweet as my mother's milk. I know that my sons and relatives too will fight among themselves and be destroyed. I cannot stop them, even as I could not stop your sons.'

Kunti came to Yudhishtira and his brothers as they were preparing to do the funeral rites and said, 'Do them for Karna as well. He was your elder brother.' And she told them the story of Karna's birth.

The Pandavas were horrified when they heard that the enemy they had feared and hated even more than Duryodhana had been their brother. They felt even worse when they heard that, apart from Arjuna, Karna had agreed to spare their lives.

After the funeral rites were completed, Yudhishtira returned to the battlefield at Kurukshetra, where Bhishma the mighty lay stoically on his bed of arrows, awaiting death. Bhishma blessed and comforted Yudhishtira, and when his time came he closed his eyes forever.

The Pandavas, Kunti and Draupadi set out for the city of Indraprastha, which had been theirs before Duryodhana had stolen it from them. They took their aged Kaurava relatives, Gandhari and Dhritarashtra, with them. Kunti devoted herself to the care of her brother-in-law and his wife. After all, they had given her shelter and taken care of her whenever her sons had been away. Saddened by the destruction and loss that the war had caused, the homecoming to Indraprastha was subdued.

The survivors of the Kurukshetra war lived
on in Indraprastha. The Kuru race, from which
they all came, had dwindled. But the race
would continue through the yet unborn son of
Abhimanyu.

This then is *Mahabharata*, the great tale of
the rulers of the kingdom of Bharata.

TAKING THINGS FURTHER

The real read

This *Real Read* version of *Mahabharata*
is a retelling of the epic originally written
in Sanskrit by Sage Vyasa. We have divided
the book into three volumes, each dealing
with different periods in the lives of the
protagonists. This is the third and final
volume, depicting the bloody battle at
Kurukshetra. The first volume deals with
the birth and childhood of the Kauravas and
the Pandavas. The second volume is about
a treacherous game of dice and its dire
consequences for the Pandavas. If you would
like to read a lengthier version of *Mahabharata*,
there are many retellings in English.

    Mahabharata is so full of stories that it
is sometimes said that if all the literature
in all the world's languages were lost, but
Mahabharata survived, it would be able to
replace all the lost stories.

Filling in the spaces

In compressing *Mahabharata* into three small volumes, we have had to omit a large portion of it. Some of the main stories we have had to leave out are mentioned here; the complete book is a never-ending source of stories.

- Hindus believe that Lord Vishnu will descend on earth as ten avatars to destroy evil and preserve dharma. He has assumed nine avatars so far, Lord Rama (see the *Real Read* version of *Ramayana*) being the seventh and Lord Krishna the ninth. The tenth is yet to come. Krishna, with his wisdom and foresight, steers the course of destiny so that dharma will eventually triumph over evil.

- The advice given by Krishna to Arjuna on the nature of karma and dharma forms the cornerstone of later Hindu philosophy. Known as the *Bhagavad Gita* or *Song of the Lord*, it includes discussions about sin and virtue, deeds and consequences, means and ends, and many other aspects of daily life. Though spiritual, the advice is also very practical.

- Parasurama, a great warrior, teaches only brahmin students. Karna pretends to be a brahmin and learns the use of weapons from him. When Parasurama learns that Karna is not a brahmin, he puts a curse on him so he will forget how to use all his special weapons when he most needs them. Karna also accidentally kills a brahmin's cow. The brahmin puts another curse on him, so the wheels of his chariot will sink into the ground at a crucial time in battle.

- In return for his earrings and armour, Karna asks Indra for a weapon that cannot be stopped. Indra gives him this weapon, but warns Karna that only one enemy can be killed with it. It is this weapon that Karna uses against Ghatotkacha. Ghatotkacha is the son of Bhima and the demoness Hidumbi, and fights so valiantly that Karna is forced to use Indra's weapon, which he had planned to use against Arjuna, against Ghatotkacha instead.

- After Abhimanyu's son grows to manhood, the Pandavas set off on the Mahaprasthana, a pilgrimage to the Himalayas which is to last until they die. On the way they are followed by a mangy dog. Draupadi becomes ill and dies, and so do the four brothers one by one, leaving only Yudhishtira and the dog. Yudhishtira is told that he can go to heaven with his earthly body, but only if he leaves the faithful dog behind. Yudhishtira refuses, but the dog reveals himself as the god of Dharma, his father, and so Yudhishtira is able to go to heaven after all.

Back in time

Ramayana and *Mahabharata* are the two epics that united India even when the country was geographically divided into a number of small kingdoms. *Ramayana* has been more popular for ritual reading, but *Mahabharata* raises questions on the nature of morality that remain provocative even today. It is the philosophical content of *Mahabharata* that places it apart.

The date of the earliest version has been placed tentatively in the eighth century BCE. The author is concerned with the nature of morality and questions the values that were taken for granted.

The author of *Mahabharata* shows that there are few clearcut solutions. Fighting should be avoided, but it becomes immoral not to fight against unacceptable exploitation and tyranny. While peace is desirable, it cannot be at any cost. Any war leaves victors looking at what they have won, and losers mourning what they have lost.

None of the characters in this story is perfect, but none is so wicked that the reader cannot find something in them to admire.

Major places and festivals

● Hastinapura, in the state of Uttar Pradesh, still exists, though today it is just a small town. It is believed that Indraprastha was located near to the city of Delhi. Kurukshetra, where the final battle took place, is in Haryana.

● Kasi or Benares, on the banks of the River Ganga, is the heart of Hinduism, and its most important pilgrimage centre.

● The most important temples dedicated to Lord Krishna in North India are at Mathura, where he was born, and at Brindavan, where he grew up.

- The temple at Dwaraka, where Krishna ruled from, is in the western state of Gujarat.

- Krishna, in the form of a child, is worshipped at Guruvayur temple in the southern state of Kerala. ISKCON, which stands for International Society for Krishna Consciousness, has temples worldwide, attracting thousands of devotees.

- Janmashtami, the festival of Krishna's birth, is celebrated each year in August or September.

- Holi, the festival of colours which is celebrated in March, is associated with Krishna's childhood.

Finding out more

Books

We recommend the following books and websites to gain a greater understanding of India and *Mahabharata*.

- Anita Vachharajani and Amit Vachharajani, *Amazing India: A State-by-State Guide*, Scholastic India, 2009.

- C. Rajagopalachari, *Mahabharata*, Bhavan's Book University, 1951.

- INTACH, *Indian Culture for Everyone*, Arvind Kumar Publishers, 2007.

- Meera Uberoi, *The Mahabharata*, Penguin Books, 2005.

- Roshen Dalal, *The Puffin History of India for Children*, Puffin Books, 2002.

- *Illustrated Guide to India*, Readers Digest in association with Penguin Books, India, 2002.

Websites

- www.gutenberg.org/ebooks/7864
The Mahabharata of Krishna-Dwaipayana Vyasa, translated into English prose by Kisari Mohan Ganguli.

- www.incredibleindia.org
A comprehensive website about India's heritage and contemporary life.

- www.intach.org
Provides useful information about the history, culture, religion and society of India.

- www.iskcon.com
Information about the Krishhna movement, which promotes the well-being of society by following Krishna's teachings.

- www.kamakoti.org
Provides detailed information about many aspects of Hinduism.

- www.krishna.com
Information about Krishna and ancient Hindu classics.

Food for thought

Mahabharata is a complex book, and rewards a full and careful reading. With the story having reached its final climax, here are some ideas for further thought and discussion.

Starting points

- What do you think was revealed about the characters in this story by the stress of war?

- The war that started out as a righteous one slowly degenerates into deceit and treachery. At what point do you think this degeneration starts?

- Do you think life was fair to Karna?

- Do you think any of the combatants regretted the war?

Themes

What do you think Vyasa says about the following themes in the context of this part of the story?

- dharma – leading a righteous life
- fate
- loyalty
- birth and lineage
- death and sorrow

Style

In many ways our *Real Read* version is very far from Vyasa's original style, but can you find examples of the following in the *Real Read* version?

- facing death
- avenging humiliation and treachery
- women and tragedy
- breaking the rules of war

Can you write a short story using some of the same ideas?

Symbols

Writers frequently use symbols in their work to deepen the reader's emotions and understanding, and Vyasa is no exception. Think about how the symbols in this list match the action in *Mahabharata*.

- light
- powerful weapons
- chariots as symbols of safety
- arrows